This Little Tiger book belongs to:

_____

_____

L. Dylan

A monster's

To Eric and Monty with love
~ TK

For Violet Léone xx
~ LS

LITTLE TIGER PRESS
1 The Coda Centre, 189 Munster Road,
London SW6 6AW
www.littletiger.co.uk

First published in Great Britain 2015
This edition published 2016
Text copyright © Timothy Knapman 2015
Illustrations copyright © Loretta Schauer 2015
Timothy Knapman and Loretta Schauer have
asserted their rights to be identified as the
author and illustrator of this work under
the Copyright, Designs and Patents Act, 1988

A CIP catalogue record for this book is available
from the British Library

Printed in China • LTP/1400/1253/1115

10 9 8 7 6 5 4 3 2 1

MOVED IN!

TIMOTHY KNAPMAN

LORETTA SCHAUER

LITTLE TIGER PRESS
London

It was summer but it was raining.
So **Barnaby** was stuck inside
with **NOTHING** to do.

"Read a book,"
said **Dad**.

"Build a rocket,"
said **Mum**.

"Go and look for dragons in the spare bedroom," said Dad.
"There's no such thing as dragons!" said Barnaby.
But then he had a BRILLIANT idea.

"I'm going to make a den,"
he said.

"But a monster might move in!"
said Mum and Dad together.

"Don't be silly!"
said Barnaby.

He made an AMAZING den.
It wasn't an outside den made of sticks and dirt and leaves.
You'd expect a **monster** to move in *there*.
It was an inside den, made of cushions
and bits of sofa, with the
rug on top. Far too cosy for

monsters.

Still, **Barnaby** got
his ray gun and his
shining armour shield,
JUST IN CASE.

But nothing the least bit exciting happened.
It just rained and rained.

Barnaby tried being a
PIRATE on the lookout
for ships to plunder . . .

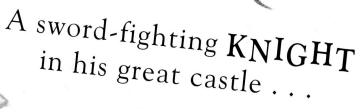

A sword-fighting KNIGHT
in his great castle . . .

A WIZARD in his cave
of wonders . . .

But it wasn't much fun on his own.
"Sometimes, I wish a monster WOULD
move in!" thought Barnaby.

BIG MISTAKE!

"I don't believe it!"
said Barnaby . . .

"A **monster's** moved in!"

"Told you so!"
said **Mum** and **Dad**.

"Grrr!"
said **Barnaby** crossly.

The **monster** didn't look very fearsome.
His T-shirt said that his name was **Burple**.
So **Barnaby** was brave and
joined him in the den.
"He seems harmless,"
thought **Barnaby**.

BIG MISTAKE!

Suddenly **Burple** started

HOWLING

so LOUDLY

that

Barnaby's

ears hurt.

Then

Burple's

DISGU

STING

PACKED LUNCH escaped
and tried to eat the den.

So they both had to sit on it
until it stopped moving.

"This is no fun at all!"
said Barnaby.

"I'm sorry but it's summer and it's
raining so there's nothing to do,"
said Burple.

That reminded **Barnaby** of
something, and he had a
BRILLIANT idea.

He read a book to Burple, and Burple said, "WOW! Let's read another!"

Then he and Burple built a rocket, and Burple said,

"COOL! Let's blast off!"

And then they went to look for DRAGONS in the spare room.

BIG
MISTAKE!

But when the smoke cleared,
Burple said,

"Yay! That was exciting!"

The rain had stopped, so they took **Burple's DISGUSTING PACKED LUNCH** for a walk in the park.

It chased sticks while they hung
upside down and told each other jokes.
Barnaby and Burple laughed so much
that their sides hurt.

Barnaby wished Burple could
stay forever.

But soon it was time
for him to go home.

"This was my best day ever!"
said Burple.

"Mine too," said Barnaby. "Thank
you for coming."

The next day, it was sunny but there was **NOTHING** to do.

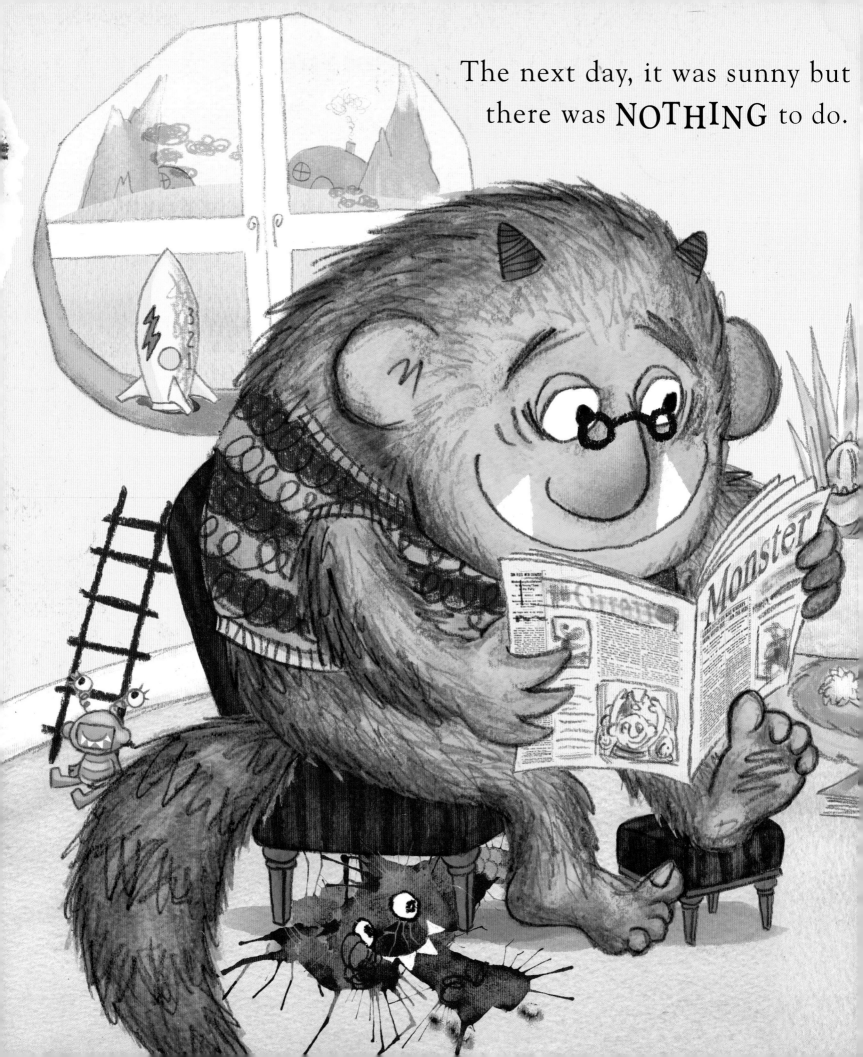

And then **Burple** had a **BRILLIANT** idea.

"I'm going to make a den,"
he said.

"But a **boy** might move in!"
said his **Mum** and **Dad** together.

"I hope so!"
said **Burple**.

And he did!

Brilliant books
to share with your
BEST BUDDIES!

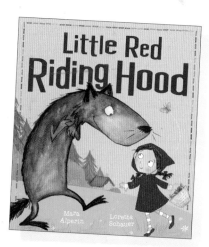

Little Red RIDING HOOD

Mara Alperin · Loretta Schauer

POO in the ZOO

Steve Smallman · Ada Grey

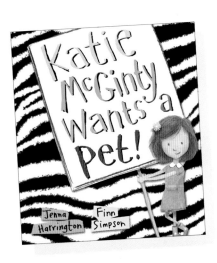

Katie McGinty Wants a Pet!

Jenna Harrington · Finn Simpson

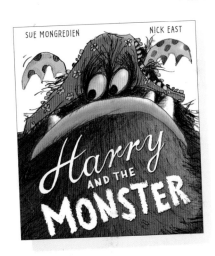

SUE MONGREDIEN · NICK EAST

Harry AND THE MONSTER

WARNING! THIS BOOK MAY CONTAIN RABBITS!

TIM WARNES

PIRATES in PYJAMAS

CAROLINE CROWE · TOM KNIGHT

For information regarding any of the above titles or for our catalogue, please contact us:

Little Tiger Press, 1 The Coda Centre, 189 Munster Road, London SW6 6AW

Tel: 020 7385 6333 • E-mail: contact@littletiger.co.uk • www.littletiger.co.uk